$= 2^{00}/LB$

$= 3^{00}/LB$

$= 3^{00}/BUNCH$

$= FREE$

CUENTO DE LUZ

To Simon and Rosemary for loving me like a daughter.
To Homeless Garden Project for filling the hearts of many people with light.
—Cristina Expósito Escalona

A New Harvest
Text © 2021 Cristina Expósito Escalona
Illustrations © 2021 Miguel Ángel Díez
© 2021 Cuento de Luz SL
Calle Claveles, 10 | Urb. Monteclaro | Pozuelo de Alarcón | 28223 | Madrid | Spain
www.cuentodeluz.com
Original title in Spanish: *Una nueva cosecha*
English translation by Jon Brokenbrow
ISBN: 978-84-18302-32-9
Printed in PRC by Shanghai Cheng Printing Company, March 2021, print number 1834-3

A New Harvest

Cristina Expósito Escalona

Miguel Ángel Díez

A tornado ripped away the soil from the ranch that Rodrigo had inherited from his parents. It was the only home he'd ever known. The wind destroyed eveything, but not Rodrigo's love for the place.

The disaster left him without a thing. A little savings, his memories, and his love for his family were the only things that kept him on his feet.

The days went by, and the soil cracked and split. It was as dry as his soul—without hope, without water, without sustenance. Rodrigo just stayed where he was.

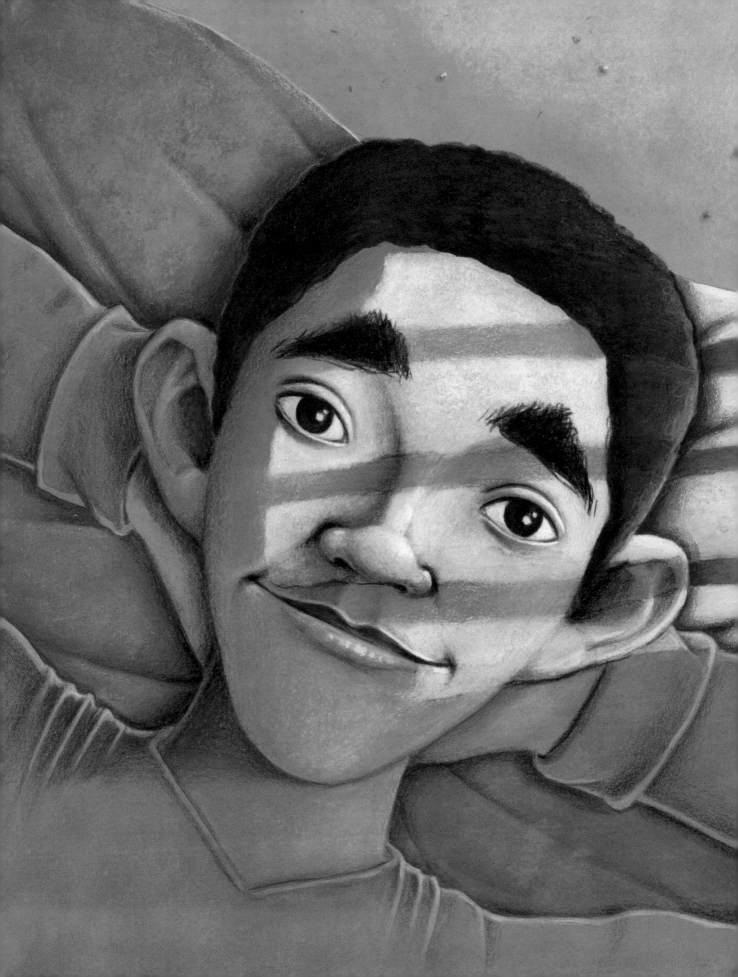

One morning, the sun woke him as it shone on his face. He remembered his father's words, the words he would repeat when things got tough.

"You've got to keep going, it's all we can do!"

And then, he felt a spark light up deep inside him.

He searched through the rubble and found the tools he'd once used on the land. He began to prepare the soil that had once supported his house. And as he dug, he found signs of life.

The following morning, he walked into town. He took some money out of his bank to buy a big bag of seeds and some new tools to make it easier to plant them.

Rodrigo worked from dawn to dusk without stopping. He carefully sowed and watered each and every seed. The plants began to grow, and at the same time, the hope and enthusiasm that made every day worth living also grew within Rodrigo.

People began to drop by, and he'd welcome them with a smile and invite them to try his organic produce. In return, they'd give him a few coins, clothes, or other things to help him out.

Over time, the land became more and more fertile. Rodrigo needed help, and the news spread like wildfire. Other people who'd lost their homes began to arrive, looking for work and food.

Little by little, Rodrigo's farm became a place where people in need came for help: a place where they could heal the wounds that nobody could see. They would lend a hand with planting the crops, they would share healthy meals, and most important of all, they would sit and listen, and give each other support.

The crops grew and grew. The farm began to supply stores and restaurants. Many people came to buy their own fruit and vegetables to eat at home.

Rodrigo and his friends used the money to build a house to shelter the workers and volunteers. There they could sleep, rest, and eat in what by now was their own home.

What had once been a small farm, and then a wasteland, had turned into the biggest project ever created by a group of homeless people. It was a place where all of them found the necessary tools to build their one true home.

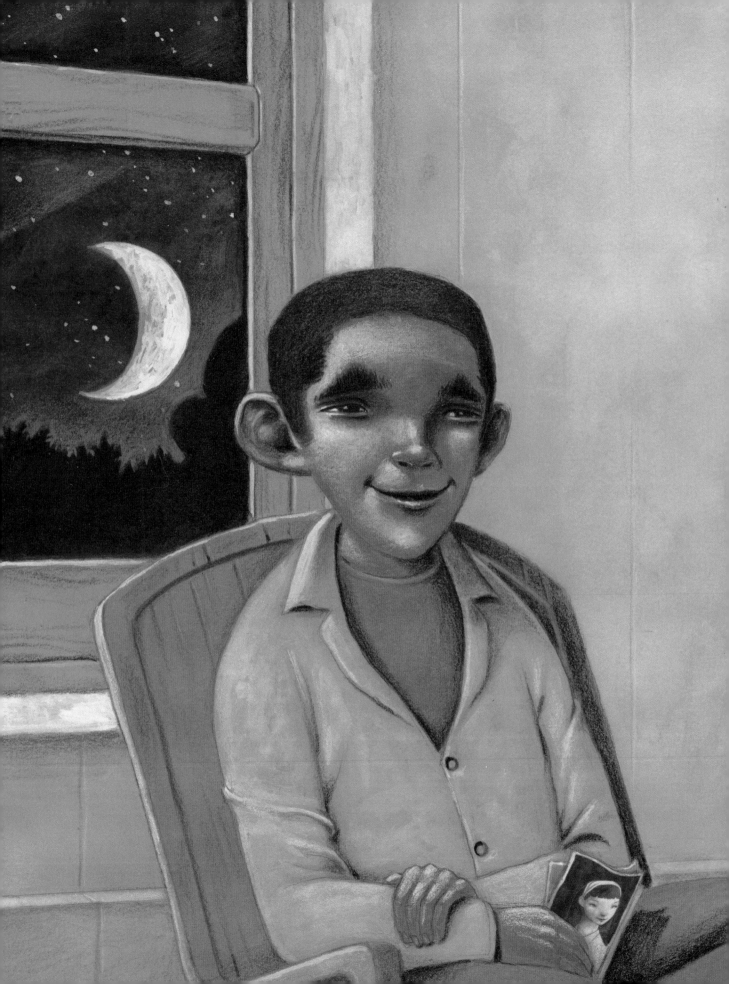

Rodrigo sat and thought about how far he'd come, and felt proud that the love for his family and the land had helped him to build a better life from the wreckage. He could provide work and shelter for people just like him, who for whatever reason had once lost everything.

ONIONS

MIXED

PEPPERS

THYME

HOPE